Get Well, Good Knight

BY Shelley Moore Thomas

PICTURES BY Jennifer Plecas

DUTTON CHILDREN'S BOOKS ◆ NEW YORK

Text copyright © 2002 by Shelley Moore Thomas
Illustrations copyright © 2002 by Jennifer Plecas
All rights reserved.

CIP Data is available.

Published in the United States 2002 by Dutton Children's Books,
a division of Penguin Young Readers Group
345 Hudson Street, New York, New York 10014
www.penguin.com
Printed in Hong Kong   First Edition
ISBN 0-525-46914-1
3 5 7 9 10 8 6 4 2

For my sister, Susan
S.M.T.

For Yona and Fred
J.P.

Once there were three little dragons.

They lived in a dark cave.

The cave was in a dense forest.

The forest was in a faraway kingdom.

The poor little dragons

were not feeling well.

They were in their beds

in the deep dark cave.

In the kingdom

there was a Good Knight.

Every night he kept watch

from his tower.

Every day he rode

in the forest.

One day he was out riding.

"Methinks I heard a sneeze,"

said the Good Knight.

He galloped through the forest.

Clippety-clop. Clippety-clop.

He came to the deep dark cave.

Inside he saw the little dragons in bed.

"What is this?" asked the Good Knight.

"Methinks my little dragon friends

are not well."

The Good Knight reached down.

He felt the dragons' scaly little foreheads.

Their heads were hot with fever.

Their noses were drip-drip-dripping.

Their teeth were chat-chat-chattering.

"Sniffle sniffle," went

the first dragon.

"Cough cough," went

the second dragon.

"Achoo!" went

the third dragon.

"Fear not, good dragons.

I will help you get well,"

said the Good Knight.

He jumped on his horse.

"Away!" he cried.

He galloped through the forest.

Clippety-clop. Clippety-clop.

He went to see the old wizard.

"I have come for help,"

said the Good Knight.

"How can I help you?"

said the wizard

in a shaky, quaky voice.

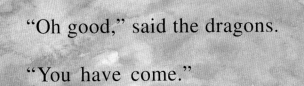

"Oh good," said the dragons.

"You have come."

"This will make you well,"

said the Good Knight.

"I have scaly snail-y soup for you."

The dragons looked at the soup.

It was dark.

It was thick.

It smelled awful.

18

"Yuck," said the dragons.

"This soup is too smelly.

We will not eat this smelly soup."

And they turned up

their little green noses.

The Good Knight did not know

what to do.

But he was a good knight.

"It can't be that bad," he said:

"I will taste it myself."

And he did.

The Good Knight's face turned pale.

He spit it out.

Pa-too-ey!

"That was bad!"

said the Good Knight.

"Sniffle sniffle," went the
first dragon.

"Cough cough," went

the second dragon.

"Achoo!" went

the third dragon.

"Fear not, good dragons.

I will help you get well,"

said the Good Knight.

He jumped on his horse.

"Away!" he cried.

He rode through the forest.

Clippety-clop. Clippety-clop.

He went back to the old wizard.

"Back again?" said the old wizard.

"How can I help you this time?"

"That soup did not help,"

said the Good Knight.

"My little dragons are still sick."

"I have just the thing,"

said the old wizard.

He got his big black pot.

He put in:

frog slime
old grime
a rusty dime
a rotten lime

He stirred the soup

round and round and round again.

"Give this to your dragons,"

said the wizard.

"It is slimy grimy soup.

This will make them well."

"Thank you. I will!"

said the Good Knight.

He rode back through the forest.

Clippety-clop. Clippety-clop.

He came to the deep dark cave.

"Oh good," said the dragons.

"You have come."

"This will make you well,"

said the Good Knight.

"Try this slimy grimy soup."

The dragons looked at the soup.

It was gooey.

It was grimy.

It looked slimy.

"Yuck!" said the dragons.

"This soup is too slimy.

We will not eat this slimy soup."

And they turned up

their little green noses.

31

The Good Knight did not know

what to do.

But he was a good knight.

"It can't be that bad,"

said the Good Knight.

"I will taste it myself."

And he did.

The Good Knight's face

turned green.

He spit out the soup.

Pa-too-ey!

"That was *really* bad!"

said the Good Knight.

"Sniffle sniffle," went the first dragon.

"Cough cough," went the second dragon.

"Achoo!" went the third dragon.

"Fear not, good dragons,"

said the Good Knight.

"I will help you get well."

The Good Knight jumped on his horse.

"Away!" he cried.

He rode through the forest.

Clippety-clop. Clippety-clop.

He did not go to see the old wizard.

He went to see his mother.

"Good day, good mother,"

said the Good Knight.

"My little dragon friends

are not well.

Can you help me?"

"You are a good knight,"

said his mother.

"You have come

to the right place.

I know just the thing."

"But that is what

the old wizard said,"

said the Good Knight.

"Mothers know best,"

said the Good Knight's mother.

She got out a pot.

She put lots of good things in it.

A little of this

and a little of that.

She stirred.

She tasted.

"Mmm," she said.

"Give this to your dragons.

This will make them well."

"Thank you, good mother.

I will," said the Good Knight.

The Good Knight

rode back through the forest.

Clippety-clop. Clippety-clop.

He came to the deep dark cave.

"Oh good," said the dragons.

"You have come."

"This will make you well,"

said the Good Knight.

"I have chicken soup for you."

"Is it smelly?" asked the dragons.

"No," said the Good Knight.

"Is it slimy?" asked the dragons.

"No," said the Good Knight.

The little dragons

looked at the soup.

It looked yummy.

It smelled yummy.

They held out their bowls.

They tasted it.

It *was* yummy.

"Yum," said the dragons.

They slurped their soup, slurp slurp.

44

They slurped until every

drop

was

gone.

"My head is not hot,"

said the first dragon.

"My nose is not dripping,"

said the second dragon.

"My teeth are not chattering,"

said the third dragon.

"We are well!" cried all three dragons.

"Thank you, Good Knight."

"Achoo!" said the Good Knight.